THIS CANDLEWICK BOOK BELONGS TO:

_____

_____

_____

_____

For John Mitchell
and Floss

First U.S. paperback edition 1994
First published in Great Britain in 1992 by
Walker Books Ltd., London.

Library of Congress Cataloging-in-Publication Data

Lewis, Kim.
Floss / Kim Lewis.—1st U.S. ed.
Summary: Even after she becomes a skilled and
hardworking sheepdog, a playful border collie never forgets
the joy of playing with happy children.
ISBN 1-56402-010-X (trade)—ISBN 1-56402-271-4 (pbk.)
[1. Border collies—Fiction. 2. Dogs—Fiction. 3. Play—Fiction.] I. Title.
PZ7.L58723Fl   1992
[E]—dc20   91-71853

4 6 8 10 9 7 5

Printed in Hong Kong

Candlewick Press
2067 Massachusetts Avenue
Cambridge, Massachusetts 02140

Floss

by Kim Lewis

CANDLEWICK PRESS
CAMBRIDGE, MASSACHUSETTS

Floss was a young
Border collie who
belonged to an old
man in a town.
She walked with the
old man in the
streets and loved
playing ball with
children in the park.

"My son is a farmer,"
the old man told Floss.
"He has a sheepdog
who is too old to work.
He needs a young dog
to herd sheep on his farm.
He could train a
Border collie like you."

So Floss and the old man
traveled, away from
the town with
its streets and houses
and children playing ball
in the park.
They came to the
heather-covered hills
of a valley, where nothing
much grew except sheep.

Somewhere in her
memory, Floss knew
about sheep.
Old Nell soon showed
her how to round them up.
The farmer trained her
to run wide and lie down,
to walk on behind,
to shed, and to pen.
She worked very hard
to become a good sheepdog.

But sometimes Floss
woke up at night,
while Nell lay sound asleep.
She remembered
playing with
children and rounding up
balls in the park.

The farmer took Floss
up to the hill one day
to see if she could gather
the sheep on her own.
She was rounding them
up when she heard a sound.
At the edge of the field,
the farmer's children were
playing with a brand-new
black-and-white ball.

Floss remembered
all about children.
She ran to play with
their ball. She showed
off her best nose kicks,
her best passes. She
did her best springs
in the air.
"Hey, Dad, look at this!"
yelled the children.
"Look at Floss!"
The sheep started
drifting away.

The sheep escaped
through the gate and
into the yard. There
were sheep in the garden
and sheep on the road.
"FLOSS! LIE DOWN!"
The farmer's voice
was like thunder.
"You are supposed to
work on this farm,
not play!"
He took Floss back to
the doghouse.

Floss lay and worried
about balls and sheep.
She dreamed about
the streets of a town,
the hills of a valley,
children and farmers,
all mixed together,
while Nell had to round
up the straying sheep.

But Nell was too old
to work every day,
and Floss had to learn to
take her place.
She worked so hard
to gather sheep well
that she was too tired
to dream any more.
The farmer was
pleased and ran Floss
in the dog trials.
"She's a good worker now,"
the old man said.

The children still wanted
to play with their ball.
"Hey, Dad," they asked,
"can Old Nell play now?"
But Nell didn't know
about children and play.
"No one can play ball
like Floss," they said.
So the farmer gave it some
thought.
"Go on, then," he whispered
to Floss.
The children kicked the
ball high into the air.

Floss remembered
all about children.
She ran to play with
their ball.
She showed off her
best nose kicks,
her best passes.
She did her best
springs in the air.
And they all played
ball together.

KIM LEWIS was born in Montreal, Canada, where she attended Concordia University and majored in printmaking. An artist and printmaker, she has had several one-woman exhibitions, and her work has been exhibited at the Royal Academy in England. Kim Lewis lives on a sheep farm in Northumberland, England, with her husband and two young children. She is the author and illustrator of several other books for young children, including *First Snow*.